Wrapped in Love

SIRIN FATHIMA

Published by SIRIN FATHIMA, 2024.

This is a work of fiction. Similarities to real people, places, or events are entirely coincidental.

WRAPPED IN LOVE

First edition. November 24, 2024.

Copyright © 2024 SIRIN FATHIMA.

ISBN: 979-8230460664

Written by SIRIN FATHIMA.

Table of Contents

CHAPTER 1 1
CHAPTER 2 7
CHAPTER 3 13
CHAPTER 4 17
CHAPTER 5 23
CHAPTER 6 29
CHAPTER 7 35
CHAPTER 8 43
CHAPTER 9 49
CHAPTER 10 55
CHAPTER 11 61
CHAPTER 12 - EPILOGUE 67

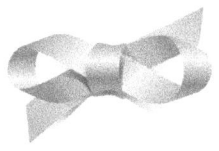

CHAPTER 1

"VED, LOOK AT THIS PHOTO. She is very pretty. She is an interior designer. You both will look together." Ved looked up at his grandmother in frustration.

How many times will he have to repeat that he isn't interested in marriage. Marriage and love are only for fools. Look at his mother. His father had destroyed her. All for love.

His mother's love for his father and his father's love for other women! It was a total disaster.

"Dadi, please don't spoil my mood in the morning." Ved said through his clenched teeth as he glared at the photos spread in front of him, wishing his eyes had the power to burn them down with a single stare.

"Oh my god! How can the faces of these pretty girls spoil your mood, Ved? They would only brighten up your day." His aunt, Daya said with a teasing smile.

"Aunt Daya, you know I am not interested in marriage. Stop forcing me for heaven sake. Please.." He pleaded looking at his aunt and grandmother and stood up to leave.

"Mayur, I am leaving for the office. Will you be joining me??" He asked his younger brother, who was still leisurely having his breakfast, enjoying his elder brother's misery.

"Of course of course I am coming," he said and they bid bye to the two ladies and also to his mother who was coming down the stairs.

She had stopped drinking after her husband's death a few months ago. And Ved hopes like hell that she wouldn't start again. He has had enough with his mother's addictions.

"Bye Maa," the brothers kissed their mother on the cheek before going out of the house.

"Karan bhaiyya called," Mayur said.

"How is bhabi's brother??" Ved asked. Karan and Naina had gone out of town for two days to visit Naina's younger brother, who is staying in a boarding school, doing his twelfth grade..

"Hale and healthy. He said they would return tomorrow evening," Mayur said.

"That's great."

Late Rajvansh Khuranna and Kalyani Khurana had two children. Dhatta Khuranna and Daya Khuranna. Dhatta got married to Ambika and Daya was married to Alok. Daya became a widow at a very young age and after her husband's untimely death, Daya returned to her parent's home with her young son, Karan. Ambika gave birth to Ved a year after Karan's birth and then to Mayur five years later. The three boys grew up together as Khuranna boys.

. . ⚜ . .

It was four in the evening and Ved felt the beginning of a migraine.

He pressed his fingers against his forehead and started massaging it to relieve the pain. It was slowly getting unbearable.

"Are you okay?" The sickeningly sweet voice reached his ears and Ved gritted his teeth in annoyance, seeing his PR head Tanya Kapoor making sheep eyes at him.

She's damn good at her work or else he would have kicked her out of his company long back.

"You want something, Tanya??" He asked in his usual cold voice he uses with people outside his family.

"I just came to show you the response to our new Villa project. The PR campaign we did in collaboration with the Talent Eye Ad Agency is a success. The bookings have already started." Tanya said smugly. Of course, the PR campaign was her idea and she would look damn smug when it got a success.

"Good," he said in a dismissive tone. What is there to be smug! He is paying her a huge amount for the work she does.

"Do you need something VK? A coffee? A painkiller? Or a massage??" Tanya asked and Ved looked at her icily.

"I need some peace which I am sure I will get once you get out of my office," he said in a dangerously calm voice.

Tanya scrambled out of his office faster than an express jet.

"I think I should just go home." Ved mumbled to himself and stood up from his chair, collecting his things.

· · ✿ · ·

Ved had taken a detour into a pocket road to avoid traffic.

He stepped on the break harshly when a whirlwind of yellow came in front of his car.

"What the hell!" He cursed as he unbuckled his seat belt and came out to see a young girl standing in front of his car, her fists clenched together and head bent down.

"Didn't you get any other vehicle to commit suicide?" He asked angrily. He was already having a headache and he didn't want to add more to it.

The girl looked up and all breath left his lungs at once. He felt a breeze skim through his skin and heard the sounds of a bell ringing. He literally felt the cupid's arrow strike square at the centre of his heart.

"Oh my god! You are so tall. And you are wearing a suit. Just like the hero in my serial," the girl said and her voice felt like music to Ved. Then he frowned as he processed her words.

"What?" He asked, confused. Serial?

"Oh lord. It's half past four already. How will I reach home in half an hour?" She talked looking backwards and that's when he realised they are in front of the Lord Shiva temple his grandmother and aunt usually comes to.

Of course that's where the bell came from, Ved. His subconscious mind said sarcastically and he ignored it.

"You need to be somewhere in half an hour urgently?" He asked curiously.

"Yes yes. It's very important that I reach home before five. But it will take more than half an hour to reach my home." She said with an adorable pout.

Ved opened his mouth to respond but she didn't let him.

"It's all because of that Munnu. He hid my sandals and I only got it now," she complained about some Munnu and Ved could only stare at the pretty girl talking to him as if he was her next door neighbour.

"Uh! I can drop you home if you want," Ved said awkwardly. He was shocked by his own words. He had never offered a girl a lift before. Not even to any acquaintances. And here, he is offering to drop a strange girl home.

"Really? You would?" He was awarded with a heart blinding smile.

"Haa," he said, quickly nodding his head.

"You are so kind," she said, looking at him with so much gratitude.

Kind? Me? Ved blinked his eyes in wonder.

"Not at all like the hero in my serial, though you both are tall, wearing suits and have big cars," she said happily skipping towards his car.

Hero in the serial? What the hell!

And how can she be so naive to get into a car with a total stranger.

What if she gets trapped with the wrong people.

Ved felt his heart stop for a moment at the thought of his sunshine girl in danger.

Your sunshine girl? How the hell did this girl become yours? His alter ego asked sarcastically and Ved again ignored it.

Ved quickly opened the car door for her and she looked up at him sadly.

"What happened??"
"I don't know how to drive a car," she said with a pout.
"It's okay. You don't have to drive," Ved said.
"Then who will drive??" She asked curiously.
"Of course I will."
"How will you drive sitting here," She asked pointing at the passenger seat and that's when it clicked Ved that she thought he opened the door for himself.

He chuckled and asked her to get in.

"Where is your home?" He asked once he got into the car and she gave him the directions. On the way, she talked nonstop, without taking a break and Ved for the first time in his life, enjoyed listening to nonsense.

They stopped near a housing colony.

"Thank-you so much. If you hadn't dropped me home I would have missed the retelecast of yesterday's episode. The thing is we have load shedding here at the time my serial is aired, so I couldn't watch it yesterday," with that said she got out of the car and skipped forwards and got lost in the crowd of people.

Ved stared at her disappearing figure in disbelief. Retelecast of a show? That was her emergency? He chuckled and then cursed himself when he realised he didn't even ask her her name.

"Damn! How will I see her again!"

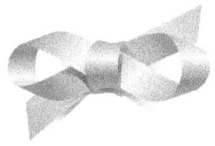

CHAPTER 2

"VED, DROP US AT THE temple." Daya asked, all ready to have an argument with her nephew to force him to drop her at the temple.

"Sure, aunt. Give me a minute. Let me change and come," he said walking towards his bedroom leaving a gaping Daya behind.

"What happened to him? I didn't even have to say it a second time.." Daya said to no one in particular. She was still in shock.

Ved quickly changed into a pair of casuals. He looked in the mirror twice before stepping out of his bedroom. It has been a week since the day he met his sunshine girl and every evening since then, he had driven back home passing through the same street where he had dropped her, taking an extra twenty minutes to reach home, in the hope that he could get a glimpse of her again.

No luck so far.

He, the eternal atheist, had passed by the Lord Shiva temple more times than he could count, hoping against hope that she would once again run into him. That didn't happen either.

It was some Teej day and the ladies in his family were fasting and his aunt had asked him to take them to the temple.

Now why in the heavens would he miss the chance to go looking for his girl again. Since it is a special day, there is a high chance that she would even be there at the temple.

"Ready??" He asked as soon as he came down all ready to go.

"You hit your head somewhere? Or are you having a fever?" Mayur asked, touching his forehead with the back of his hand.

"Shut up, Mayur." He said angrily, trying to hide his embarrassment. In the excitement of going and meeting his girl, he had forgotten that his family would definitely notice the change in his behaviour.

"Come ,let's go," Ambika said with a soft smile.

There's something different in her son's behaviour and she hopes it's for good.

．． ⚜ ．．

The ladies had gone into the temple and Ved had wandered around the temple for the better part of an hour and finally accepted defeat.

He is not going to find her, he thought and sat on the steps leading to the temple pond.

As he sat lost in thoughts, he felt a pair of soft hands covering his eyes.

"Guess who?" The angelic voice spoke and Ved felt his heart beat faster. He would recognise that voice anywhere, anytime.

"You didn't tell me your name that day," he said, smiling like a fool.

"Neither did you tell me your name.?" She said, taking her hands off his eyes and sitting next to him.

"You didn't ask..!" He said with a wide smile.

"Uh oh! I didn't, did I? I was so caught up with the tension that I wouldn't reach home by the time the series started that I forgot everything else.." She said, slapping her own head a couple of times.

"Haa. Your series. You watched it that day. You didn't miss it, right?" Ved asked curiously.

"No! I was right on time. Only because of you. You are so sweet," She said, shooting a heart smile his way and Ved wondered what his employees would think if they ever heard this girl call him sweet.

"But I will miss it today," she said with a sad pout.

"Why will you miss it?? There's enough time for you to reach home before five." Ved said, looking at his wrist watch, although he doesn't want her to go home yet. He wanted to keep listening to her musical voice.

"No! Today is Teej. I am fasting. I have to stay here at the temple till the moon comes. And by the time the moon comes, the showtime will be over. I will miss this one episode. Tomorrow onwards the power shedding timings change. Thank god." She said with a sigh of relief.

"You are also fasting?" Ved asked.

"Yes yes. My mama is a Shiva worshipper. So, she wanted me to keep fast today." She said with a pout.

"Mama said .. 'Geet, no matter how much you pout, you will have to keep fast. I am not going to let you eat anything until the moon comes out' " She said, imitating her mother.

Geet... his heart whispered with a smile.

"Teej is celebrated in dedication to Maa Parvati's love for Shiva. It's said that Maa Parvati fasted and fasted for years and finally in her 108th birth Lord Shiva accepted her as his wife." Geet added the story her mama tells her every year during this day.

"Oh! That's some love," Ved said not knowing how to respond to that.

"I know right! Maa said if I also keep fast ,I will also get a husband like Lord Shiva." She said, happily informing him that she is waiting for her own Prince Charming.

"Maybe your fasting worked. I am Ved. My dadi always says I have all the qualities of Lord Shiva." Ved said cheekily and Geet giggled at his comment.

A few seconds later, Ved saw her staring into the pond, lost in her own thoughts. He snapped his fingers in front of her, startling her.

"Uh?"

"Where are you lost, Geet?" Ved asked, seeing her dazed look.

"Oh, I was thinking about my series. Yesterday, the hero made the heroine cry. He is such an arrogant man.." Geet said, huffing in annoyance.

Ved cringed realising that is one word people always use when describing him.

"Why did he make her cry?" Ved asked curiously, just because he wanted to listen to her talks.

"Oh! You want to know the whole story so far? I will tell you.." Geet said excitedly. She just loves talking about her favourite series.

"Uh yeah!!"

"My hero.. He is very arrogant and rude. He doesn't believe in love and marriages. He is so cold hearted. He is very rich and the girl is...."

"Very poor?" Ved asked, before Geet could complete her sentence.

"How do you know? Do you also watch my series?" Geet asked, narrowing her eyes at him.

"Of course not." Ved said, offended that anybody could think that he watches stupid ITV shows.

"The hero, he had a very difficult..."

"Past? Childhood?" Ved asked once again, breaking Geet's words.

"You watch my series. I am sure." Geet accused angrily.

"No, I don't." Ved said in a helpless tone.

"Then how are you telling the story of my series?" Geet asked suspiciously.

"What is there to know? This is what has been happening in ITV shows since forever." Ved mumbled, remembering all the daily soap operas he had to watch sitting with his Aunt Daya during his childhood days.

"I won't talk to you. You watch my series and yet you couldn't even tell me what happened in the yesterday's episode" Geet pouted

"Geet, I don't watch series. And if you want you can watch it on your phone. Do you have a phone Geet?" Ved asked and Geet grinned happily.

"Yes, yes, I do. Papa said, in cities everyone has a phone, so I should also have one. He bought me a new one when we came to the city." Geet said excitedly and took her phone and showed it to him, which was a base model phone.

"Oh! You can't watch in this" Ved said in disappointment.

"We can only watch on those big phones that my hero and heroine uses??" Geet asked curiously and a tad bit sadly.

"Yes, you need smart phones for that. Wait a minute," Ved took out his spare phone which he usually uses for personal purposes and removed his sim card.

He then asked her in which channel she watches the series, before installing the corresponding application on the phone.

"Keep it," he said and gave it to her.

"For me?" Geet asked happily and checked the phone, turning it up and down.

"Yes," he said and a few seconds later her smile dimmed.

"Momma will scold me. And I don't even know how to use it." Geet said sadly, extending the phone back to him.

"I will teach you. And you don't have to tell your mom. Hide it," Ved said and his conscience chided him for spoiling the innocent girl.

"Hide from momma? Oh it would be interesting," Geet said chirpily.

Ved took out the wireless wifi router from his pocket and handed it to her and explained to her how to switch it on and how to connect the wi fi to her phone.

Then he opened the channel application and asked her the name of the show she watches.

Once she told him the name of the show, he searched for it and opened it, and showed it to her. And the smile on her face was worth all the effort.

"Hayee... I can watch all these?? From the very first episode??" Geet asked happily and in disbelief.

"Yes. You can," he said and then he deleted his WhatsApp account from the phone and created an account with her phone number.

"This is WhatsApp. And this is my number. I have saved it here. So you can message me anytime you want. And see this. You can press here to call me. And if you want to see me you can press this video icon and we can talk on a video call, seeing each other." Ved explained to her the things he so badly wanted to do.

"Wow. This is so awesome. We don't have the internet and stuff in our village. Even the TV signals sometimes go off." Geet informed him about the remote part of her village.

"Oh it's time for the puja. I should go," Geet said as she heard the bell ring at the temple.

"Oh! Will you call me at night Geet??" He asked, feeling stupid like a teen-ager asking his crush out for the first time.

"You want me to?" Geet asked with her wide innocent eyes.

"Yes," there was no need for a second thought.

"Then I will call you. I will also tell you what happened in my series" she said and skipped back to the temple leaving a smiling Ved behind.

"Hayee!! My heart!" Ved said, clutching his heart, with a dazed look on his face.

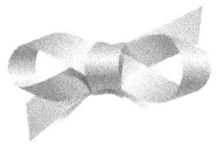

CHAPTER 3

VED WALKED INTO THE temple, his eyes roaming around to find his sunshine girl, but he couldn't see her anywhere!

Where did she disappear so fast?

He was looking around when he felt someone tap on his shoulder. He turned around with a wide smile, which dimmed when he saw who it was.

"Ved? You are still here?? You haven't gone home yet??" Daya asked suspiciously.

"Wo- I was looking- er - I was looking at the temple architecture." Ved stammered and came up with a stupid excuse.

"Temple architecture? Why?" Daya asked in confusion.

"Uh aunt, I was planning to build a temple," he blurted out and Daya's eyes widened when she heard his words.

"Oh my God! For which goddess are you building the temple for?" Daya asked teasingly.

"Haha... Build means, I heard about a government tender on rebuilding an old temple. I was looking around ,so that I could get a better idea to make a decision." Ved said without meeting his aunt's eyes.

"Really? Why do I feel like you are lying to me?" Daya asked suspiciously.

"I am getting late, aunt. I got a call from the office now. I have to go." He said and made his escape from there quickly, disappointed that he couldn't say a bye to Geet before leaving.

He got into his car and took deep breaths to calm himself.

"Relax Ved!! You can talk to her at night. She promised to call," he spoke to himself, before starting the car and speeding off.

"I am done. Goodnight everyone." Ved said getting up from the dining room.

"Pool side??" Karan asked, making sure that they will be having their usual brother's only meet by the pool side at night.

"Uh. Not today, Karan. I have a headache.Let me sleep it off," With that said he dashed off to his room and locked it not wanting to risk Mayur barging in later.

Ved paced the room for an hour waiting for the call.

"Why is she not calling?? Did she forget about me?? Should I call her and check? No no, Ved. What if she is with her parents. I should have asked her at what time she is going to call. Maybe she fell asleep." Ved talked to himself realising it was close to midnight.

His phone rang at that moment and Ved picked up at the first ring.

"Geet??"

"Ved ji.. " she whispered softly.

Ved smiled contently, and leaned back on the recliner in his room.

"Did you have dinner, Geet?" He asked tenderly.

"Haa.." She whispered again.

"Why are you whispering?" He asked curiously.

"If I talk loudly, momma and papa will wake up," she whispered again.

"You are sleeping with your parents?" He asked in disbelief.

"No. They are in the next room. But we can hear what we talk. I can always hear them talking in the next room, while sitting here. So they must also be able to hear me if I talk, right?" She whispered.

"Oh, I see."

"And it's very hot too. Inside the blanket," she complained.

"Why are you inside the blanket if it's hot?" Ved asked, totally confused.

"I am hiding inside, Ved ji. What if papa or momma comes at night to check on me hearing any noise. If I am inside the blanket, I can easily hide the phone." She said cheekily.

"Ah ha!! Where did you get this idea from, Geet? I thought you were such an innocent girl." Ved said in amusement

"Me? Innocent? Hayee. You come and tell my momma this one day okay. She always says I am the devil's own pawn. You come and tell my mama that I am very sweet, cute and innocent." Geet whispered and Ved laughed loudly.

"Are you making fun of me?" She whispered angrily and he could picture her pouting cutely.

"No baby. You tell me, why are you so late? What were you doing?" Ved asked curiously.

"My show is at half past ten at night. It only got over by eleven." Geet whispered.

"And it's twelve now. What were you doing for one hour?" There was a note of complaint in Ved's voice.

"About that, after the episode got over, I felt like watching it again. So, I watched it in that application you showed me today. When I saw that episode, I felt like, watching their first meeting. So, I watched that episode too before calling you," Geet whispered and Ved shook his head in disbelief.

Here he was pacing around waiting for her call and she was busy watching her serial.

"Did you watch to your heart's content?" He asked with a fond smile.

"No, Ved ji." She said in a disappointed tone.

"Why not?"

"I told you, right. Mama and Papa can hear from the other room. So, I watched the show on mute."

"Oh. No worries, you meet me at the temple tomorrow evening. I will give you my headphones."

"Another phone?"

"No no. Headphone means, we connect it to the phone and place it in our ears so that only we can hear." Ved explained gently.

"Oh, the ones with long wires? I have seen it on TV. Nobody uses these in our village." Geet said.

"That's okay, Geet. I will teach you everything about city life. So when will you come to the temple?" He asked all excited to meet her again.

"At five?"

"Okay,"

"Oh Ved ji, I totally forgot. I didn't tell you what happened in the serial today." Geet said excitedly.

"Haa. Tell me," he said, ready to listen to any nonsense as long as it was her voice.

She spoke elaborately when speaking about her favourite show and her favourite hero and heroine.

"And then this villain.. He is obsessed with the heroine." Geet said.

"Obviously.." Ved murmured rolling his eyes, wondering when the Indian TV industry was going to bring in some new plot.

And the conversation went on for sometime.

"Then what happened?" Ved asked and only heard the soft breathing from the other side as a response.

Ved looked at the time and realised it was half past one..

"Goodnight, love." He whispered and hung up the call and lied down to sleep with a soft smile on his lips.

CHAPTER 4

"KHANNA? IS THE CONFERENCE room ready?" Ved asked the Khuranna's second in command

"Yes sir. The meeting starts in ten minutes. All the department heads are already in the conference room." Khanna said.

"Cool. Let's get going." Mayur said and the three Khuranna brothers walked towards the conference room for the monthly meeting with the department heads.

"Good Morning all," The meeting began shortly.

"Ms Kapoor. The PR campaign for the villa project has been a success. Keep up the work. And keep working with the same Advertising agency for the future projects too," Karan said appreciating Tanya Kapoor for her recent good job.

"Thank-you KK." Tanya said smugly.

"It seems all the villas are already booked. Mr Mathur, hire the best interior designer. The construction works are almost over. Contact the buyers and ask their opinion about the interiors. Make sure not to change the base our interior designer made. Give preference to fresh candidates. Offer an internship for three months and permanent job in our team only if they prove themselves," Ved said.

"Noted VK" Akshay Mathur said, noting it down on his notepad quickly.

"Who is dealing with the Government tender?" Mayur asked and Ved looked at him in shock.

Did Aunt Daya ask him about the temple renovation he lied about?

"Huh Mayur...it was a rumour. I confirmed," Ved said, making his brothers frown in confusion.

"It's not a rumour, Ved. It's legit. Didn't you check the file?" Karan asked suspiciously.

"What file?" Ved asked, clueless.

"The file I gave you last night after dinner." Karan reminded him.

Damn!!

The file he couldn't check because Geet called him earlier than usual because he had subscribed to the premium in the channel application for the exact same purpose.

"Oh yes yes. The Government Tender," Ved said, making his brothers give him odd looks.

What happened to you? They seem to ask through their eyes which Ved decided to ignore.

"So who is dealing with it??" Ved asked, recovering his composure soon.

"I am in charge, VK." Mr Roy said.

The meeting was disrupted by the loud shrill of a phone.

'Jhoome Jo Pathaan Meri Jaan,

Mehfil Hi Loot Jaaye,

Dede Jo Zubaan Meri Jaan,

Uspe Mar Mit Jaaye'

"What the!" Everyone went silent as the phone rang in the conference room.

"Don't you know to keep the phone in silent mode while in the conference room??" Ved asked no one in particular.

Mayur nudged him with the elbow.

"Ved, It's your phone," Mayur said, still trying to recover from the shock of the ringtone.

Since when did Ved become a Sharukh Khan fan? Since when did Ved start watching Bollywood movies? When did Ved start listening to bollywood songs? Any songs at that?

"Mine?" Ved asked in horror and took the phone which was kept upside down on the desk.

Geet! The caller ID read.

When did she change the ringtone of his phone?

She did use his phone yesterday when they met at the temple. Did she change the ringtone then? But she had called him last night and it was the usual ringtone.

He disconnected the call and was about to activate the do not disturb mode when he realised it's already activated.

Then how the hell did the phone ring?

It was followed by a text message which was simply a sad face smiley from Geet.

Ved groaned mentally. How can he concentrate on the meeting now?

"Excuse me!! This is important," Ved excused himself and walked out of the conference room, leaving everyone shocked.

What is more important than a meeting for VK, the workaholic, the question seems to linger in everyone's mind.

Ved dialled Geet's number who picked up the call on the first ring.

"Apni Kurse Ke Paite Baandh Lo... Mausam Bigadne Wala Hai" Geet said, all in the Sharukh Khan style.

"What?" Ved asked bewildered.

"Why didn't you pick up when I called??" Geet asked with an angry pout.

"I am at work, Geet. I was in a meeting" Ved said softly.

"Uh oh. Sorry Ved ji. I forgot you went to work. Did your boss scold you? If he did, you tell him you know Geet. In my village, everyone tells me that I am a gundi. I can very well deal with your boss." Geet said and Ved chuckled at her cuteness.

"No one scolded me. Now tell me why did you change my ringtone? And how come I didn't realise it until now??"

"That's a special ringtone for my calls only, Ved ji. You hear it only when I call you. I learned it on my phone. And I was checking whether I can do it on your phone too." Geet said chirpily.

"Then why didn't I hear it when you called me last night?" Ved asked in confusion.

"Uffo. You are such an idiot. Yesterday I called you on WhatsApp. It was an internet call. Today I called you from my mobile. My small one." Geet said, explaining it to Ved.

Within a week Geet became an expert in everything related to smart phones and she is the one now teaching new things to Ved.

"From your mobile. Wah!! What happened that you are calling me so bravely during the day??" Ved teased.

"Momma and Papa have gone out. Papa got a new contract with a big company. We will be making breakfast, lunch and evening snacks for the company. Papa said it's going to be wonderful. So they have gone out for grocery shopping" Geet said.

It has become a habit for her to share anything and everything happening in her life with Ved.

She wouldn't be at peace until she shares things with Ved.

How did she live the last twenty years, Geet wondered.

Last night she even had a dream in which she and Ved were dancing instead of Sharukh Khan and Kajal in the 'suraj hua mad ham' song.

Geet blushed hard at the thought and she suddenly felt shy to talk to him.

"Okay, I am hanging up," she hung up, blushing profusely

Oh god, Geet. Vedji is your friend. How can you have such inappropriate thoughts about him?

Ved frowned at the phone?

What happened to her all of a sudden?

Why did she hang up like that??

He opened the messaging app and decided to send her a text.

'Five in the evening?. Near the temple??' He asked and waited for her response.

Mayur walked into his elder brother's cabin only to see him staring at the phone

"Ved?"

"Huh?"

"You said you had an important call. And here you are staring at your phone?"

"I just hung up the call and I am waiting for an important email. What are you doing here? Don't you have any work to do? Why are you wasting my time here?" Ved asked angrily.

Offence is the best form of defence and Ved decided to go forward with it

"Something is off with you Ved. I should ask Aunt Daya to ward off evil eyes." Mayur said and Ved rolled his eyes.

Nothing is off with him.

Everything just started getting ON.

CHAPTER 5

"UNCLE JI, ONE MORE please. Make it extra spicy." Geet told the street vendor, Gupta ji, selling pani puris.

"Here, Geet bitiya," the man made a plate of spicy pani puris and handed it over to the young girl.

The girl and her family recently moved to their housing colony. The people living here in this colony have been here for years and they were a close knit unit. So when Shukla ji informed them about renting one of his houses to a family migrating from a distant village, they were all apprehensive of letting new people in. They didn't want any sort of disturbances.

But Geet with her sunny nature, bright smile and chirpy talks won the hearts of them all within a matter of few days.

Yesterday Shuklaji even talked about asking her hand in marriage for his son.

But Gupta didn't want that to happen.

Geet bitiya is too young to be married to Shukla's son. Moreover Geet bitiya is too beautiful for Shukla's son. Geet bitiya deserves nothing less than a charming prince.

"This is so tasty, Gupta uncle ji. I will come again tomorrow. Here," Geet said and extended her hands with the three twenty rupees notes.

"Keep it bitiya. It's free for you today." Gupta said with a fond smile.

"Momma will scold me uncle ji.." She said with a pout and Gupta reluctantly took the money.

"Geet didi! Geet didi!" A little boy, a member of Geet's kiddo gang in the colony came running to her all breathless.

"Chintu? What happened? Why are you running like this?" Geet asked.

"Nalini aunty is calling you home. Haresh uncle met with an accident." Chintu said breathlessly.

"Papa..." Geet cried and ran to her home, only to see her father sitting with his bandaged legs propped up on the tea table.

"Papa, what happened?" Geet ran to him crying.

"Nothing, Chutki. Papa is okay. I just fell down and sprained my ankle. Doctor saab said a few days of rest will cure it." Haresh said softly.

"How did you fall?? You should always be careful papa." Geet chided her father for his carelessness.

"Okay darling. Sorry, I will be careful from now on." Haresh promised his daughter, who was glaring down at him now.

"Haresh ji. Drink this." Nalini Jha, Greg's mother, handed over a glass of homemade concoction to her husband as a remedy for his pain.

"Nalini, if the lunch boxes are ready, Lal will be here in an hour. You go with him." Haresh said, worried about their new clients.

Usually it's him who takes the food to the Khuranna Industries. As he couldn't move his leg for a few days, he asked Lal, the rickshaw driver living in their colony to take his wife to the office to deliver the food.

· · ✧ · ·

An hour later.

Geet tried to take her father to the bedroom so that he can rest, but she wasn't strong enough to support him.

Nalini came forward and helped them.

"Geet, do one thing. You go with Lal ji." Nalini said, shocking both father and daughter.

"Nalini, she is a child. How will she manage alone?" Haresh asked worriedly.

"Haresh ji. We are in the city now. We need to let her do things on her own. Else she wouldn't be able to cope in the city." Nalini said and

Haresh knew it was true. This place is so different from the village they had lived in all these years.

"Papa. I am a big girl. I can manage." Geet said, frowning at her father for calling her a child.

"Chutki. I am just worried. It's a big company. Be careful, okay. I have heard the bosses of the company are very rude and arrogant. If one mistake happens ,they will cancel our contract." Haresh said, anxiously.

"Don't worry papa. I won't make any mistakes." Geet promised.

"I hope you won't bump into KK or VK." Haresh said, making Geet frown.

"KK and VK??" She asked with a confused frown on her face.

"Yeah. They are the bosses," Haresh said and Geet broke into a fit of laughter.

"What strange names they have, papa. Who names their children KK and VK?" Geet asked, laughing at the hilarity.

"Don't go there and say this Geet." Haresh warned his daughter who has no control over her tongue.

. . ༄ . .

Geet stepped out of the rikshaw and looked at the skyscraper building in awe.

"OMG! How big is this building?" She gaped at the very tall building with her wide eyes.

"They are one of the richest families in India, Geet. Very powerful too." Lal said, taking the boxes out of the rikshaw, helping Geet.

They reached the canteen and saw a lady shouting at another lady.

"What do you mean by lunch has not arrived yet. There's an important meeting in an hour. It's your responsibility to make sure the office cafe runs smoothly. You are not paid for nothing," the lady shouted and Geet shuddered hearing it.

'Today you are gone Geet Jha. What was the need to stop in between to buy the cotton candy? Papa had warned you not to make any mistakes and see what you did?' Geet spoke to herself.

"Hello Madam, I am Geet Jha. Haresh Jha's daughter," she introduced herself to the lady who was screaming a moment ago.

"So?" The rude lady asked, looking at her in disgust.

"We came with lunch, Madam. What happened is, papa got into-" she was rudely cut off by the lady standing in front of her.

"So, you are that irresponsible idiot who couldn't do the job they are hired for properly?" The lady shouted at her angrily.

Geet gulped in fear. Nobody has ever screamed at her like this.

"Sorry madam ji. I was..-"

"Shut up. Don't know who hired you. And what the hell are you wearing?" The lady looked at her outfit with evident distaste.

Geet looked down at herself.

She is wearing one of her favorite outfit. A yellow kamiz with red salwar with all the pompoms attached to it.

Her eyes filled up and tears started running down her cheeks listening to the lady still shouting at her

"Tanya ,that's enough," Mayur who came down for lunch said not liking the way Tanya was bullying the girl who seems like she would burst out into loud sobs any moment.

"MK. If we don't point out their mistakes, they will take it for granted and repeat it." Tanya said.

"Stop it Tanya. Bhai is coming down for lunch. Don't bring this into his attention. The girl is already crying. If bhai says something she will definitely faint or something." Mayur warned her about Ved.

"VK is coming?? Great." Tanya looked at Geet and smirked.

Maybe this is an opportunity to impress VK. To let him know that PR is not the only field she could deal with. If he marries her, she could stand by his side and help him run the company smoothly.

Ved walked into the cafe only to see a group of people surrounding someone.

"What's happening here?" He asked no one in particular and the people moved aside, giving him a way.

Geet, who was having palpitations at the mention of the rude arrogant VK, heard the very familiar voice and turned around to see her Ved ji standing there.

A big smile broke out on her face realising that she is not alone.

"Ved ji," she called out loudly and ran to him and hugged him tightly.

Ved froze for a moment along with all the others in the cafe.

Everyone held their breath waiting for the explosion.

A chit of a girl had dared to hug VK. And dared to call him Ved ji.

The girl is dead today.

But to their utter shock, VK wrapped his arms around the still trembling girl and looked down at her face.

They stared transfixed seeing the always thunderous face softening. The eyes that always spit fire at them turned tender when he looked at the girl in his arms.

Are they dreaming??

Did VK go mad??

Or is it them who went mad??

Ved's breath hitched seeing the tear stained face of his Geet.

"Geet, why are you crying? What happened, bacchha?" He asked, wiping her tears with his thumbs.

"I am so happy you are here. I was so scared that VK would come and scold me. Do you know VK, Ved ji. Please tell him I didn't come late intentionally. Papa fell down and sprained his ankle. That's why I had to come." Geet said in between her hiccups.

"Relax, bachha. It's okay, it's okay. Come with me," he took her hands and guided her to the elevator to take her to his cabin.

"Somebody, pinch me please." Mayur whispered and Drishti who stood next to him pinched him hard.

Mayur hissed.

"Who was that??" Mayur asked, still in daze.

"Geet. That's what she said," Drishti said, still staring into the space they had occupied a moment ago.

"Not the girl. Who is that guy? That couldn't be my brother. No way!" Mayur mumbled more to himself.

He had no idea what all they were going to witness in the coming days!!

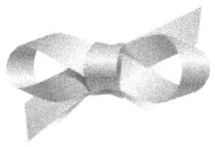

CHAPTER 6

VED TOOK GEET TO HIS cabin and made her sit on the couch in the corner. He then kneeled in front of her and wiped her ever running tears.

"What happened Geet. Why were you crying?" Ved asked gently

"I was so scared. Papa said if any mistake happens, VK and KK will cancel our contract. I didn't mean to come late, Ved ji." Geet said in between her hiccups.

"It's okay, bachha. Now stop crying please. I don't feel good when you cry, Geet." Ved said sadly.

"I am not crying. My eyes are just sweating," Geet said, wiping her tears.

"Really? And I remember someone telling me that they were scared," Ved teased.

"That Tanya madam ji looked really scary."

Tanyaa, you will pay for this. You will pay for making my girl cry, Ved gritted his teeth angrily..

"I thought such people only exist in movies and serials. Do you know, she looks so much like my hero's ex-girlfriend who is also the villain in the serial." Geet said in a hushed whisper.

"She kept on shouting," Geet complained.

"Really? And where did the Gundi Geet go when she was shouting? I wonder if she really is really a gundi as she claims to be." Ved teased her again.

Geet huffed in annoyance.

"That's because I was caught off guard. I didn't expect to meet someone like that. If I see her ever again, I will kick her so hard that she will never forget me ever again." Geet vowed.

"That's like my Geet." Ved said, pulling her cheeks.

"Ved ji, iit hurts." Geet said, rubbing her cheeks.

"Okay, now tell me what happened to papa??" Ved asked seriously.

"He is so careless. He fell down and sprained his ankle. So I came here with Lal ji..- Hai bhagwan! Lal ji is waiting for me outside Ved ji. I have to go." Geet sprang up from the couch, all ready to run downstairs.

"Geet," Ved held her hands stopping him.

"Yes, Vedji" Geet smiled at him and Ved felt that his heart would burst out any minute. He was not able to handle such strong and intense emotions.

"Don't ever cry, okay?" He said cupping her face.

"Hmmm,"

"If someone says something to you, you tell me, okay? I will deal with them." Ved said and pressed a feather light kiss on her forehead shocking her.

Geet's eyes widened and she gaped at him with an open mouth.

Ved chuckled at her expression which bought Geet out of her shock. She looked down shyly, blushing furiously.

"You are so cute," Ved said and Geet ran out of the cabin, Ved following behind with a silly grin on his face.

．．⚘．．

"Khanna, take these files to the Architecture department." Karan handed over the files to Khanna and walked towards his brother's cabin.

As he neared the cabin, he saw a girl sitting there and crying?

What the hell?

Who is she and how dare she enter VK's cabin without permission?

He strode forwards, all set to blast her for trespassing and that's when he saw his brother kneeling in front of her.

What the f*ck!

Karan rubbed his eyes to clear his vision to make sure he is not hallucinating.

No!! He is not!

It's his brother only. Or a doppelganger of his brother. Because there is zero percent chance of his brother kneeling down in front of any girl.

But then that's not literally possible. Doppelgangers exists only in movies and television shows.

It's the VK. The same VK who runs a mile if he so much as hears about a crying woman.

The very same VK is sitting there and wiping an unknown girl's tears.

Karan's eyes widened even more when he saw Ved pull her cheeks, with a besotted smile on his face..

What the actual f*ck!

Then they talked about something and the girl sprang up from the couch and ran towards the cabin door only to be stopped by his brother.

Karan saw Ved cupping her face and looking tenderly at her.

What the bloody f*ck!

Then he saw Ved kissing her forehead.

What the ever loving f*ck!

Karan realised he had never cursed this much in his life before.

"Am I dreaming bhaiyya?" Karan looked beside him to see Mayur too gaping at the duo inside Ved's cabin.

The cabin door opened and a whirlwind of yellow ran out only to stop abruptly in front of them.

The silly grin present on Ved's face vanished as soon he took in his brothers' presence.

Damn!!

He hadn't even bothered about his employees watching when he took Geet to his cabin.

All that mattered at that time was that his girl was crying and he needed to console her.

"Namaste," Geet folded her hands in front of the two men and they in turn folded their hands in daze.

Ved looked surprised seeing Karan folding his hands in namaste. If he wasn't the one caught, he would have laughed at the scene unfolding in front of him.

"Geet. Let's go," Ved said, trying to get her away from his brothers.

"Wait a second, Ved ji. Let me thank MK ji. He helped me downstairs," Geet said and shot a bright smile at Mayur.

"Thank you so much MK ji, for trying to save me from that horrible lady, uh, I mean Tanya ji," Geet said with a sheepish smile.

"It's okay," Mayur said, still confused as to who she is.

"By the way, can I ask you something?" She asked curiously and Mayur nodded.

"Why do you have such a strange name? Before coming here, I had heard about KK and VK. Papa said that they are very arrogant and rude and that I should be careful not to cross paths with them. But you are very sweet, MK ji. Why do you have a name like them?" Geet asked curiously.

Does Geet's father think like that about him? Ved wondered anxiously.

I have to do something about this, he thought to himself.

Karan frowned hearing the girl call him arrogant. He opened his mouth to retort when he saw his brother glaring at him.

"You can call me Mayur." Mayur said and Geet gasped.

"Mayur bhaiyya?? Ved ji's younger brother? Why didn't you tell me before?" Geet asked excitedly, happy to meet the Mayur she has heard a lot about.

"You know me?" Mayur asked in surprise.

"Of course. Vedji has told me lots and lots about you. He said you are such a troublemaker." Geet laughed.

"Really?" Mayur said, raising an eyebrow at his elder brother, Ved, who refused to look at him.

"I am Karan." Karan introduced himself, not liking the fact that Ved didn't talk about him to this girl.

"Bade bhaiyya?" Geet smiled brightly at him.

"Yes!"

"Naina bhabhi is right. You are really a cat. You have blue eyes.." Geet said looking at Karan's blue eyes in awe/

"She knows Naina too??" Karan asked in surprise.

"Arre I know everyone. Waise Ved ji never said you all are working in the same company!" Geet said, pouting at Ved for keeping that secret from him.

"Geet, Lal ji must be waiting. Let's go." Ved tried to hurry Geet out of the office.

"Oh Ved ji, I forgot again. Poor Lal ji must be really bored now, waiting for me. Bhaiyyas, I will meet you again soon. Oh by the way, why don't you two come to the temple with Ved ji in the evening? We can talk a lot peacefully." Geet said, with wide hopeful eyes.

"Ved is coming to meet you this evening?" Karan asked, shooting a look at Ved..

"We meet every day, right Ved ji?" Geet asked and looked at Ved to see him looking frustrated.

"Are you hiding this from your family too, Vedji?? But I thought we were only hiding from my parents. You didn't tell me it was a secret." Geet said apologetically.

"That's okay Geet. Come let's go." Ved said in exasperation.

"Okay," Geet nodded and Ved guided her towards the elevator.

As the elevator door was closing, Mayur called out to them.

"See you at the temple in the evening, Geet."

CHAPTER 7

VED WALKED BACK TO his cabin with a lazy smile, which vanished the second he saw his brothers waiting for him there.

"I have a client meeting now. I guess, see you at home." Ved said, turning on his heels, all set to walk out of the office to escape from his brothers' third degree.

"Home? So you are not coming with us to the temple this evening?" Mayur asked, folding his arms across his chest.

Ved stared at him in horror.

"You are not serious??" Ved asked in disbelief.

"Of course I am. First time, bhabhi invited me somewhere. How can I not go." Mayur said cheekily.

Bhabhi, He liked the sound of that.

Karan choked on air seeing his brother's cheek turn slightly red.

"Are you? Are you blushing, Ved??" Karan couldn't believe his eyes. The Ved Khuranna is blushing?

"What?? No!! Of course No!" Ved denied vehemently.

"You totally are.." Mayur said scrutinising him more.

"Now tell us all about your Geet." Karan demanded.

Ved sighed realising he couldn't hide it from his brothers anymore.

He proceeded to tell them how he met her through an almost accident. How he dropped her home. And how he met her again at the temple. How they became friends. And how he fell in love with her more and more with each passing second.

Ved had a dreamy look on his face while talking about Geet.

"Love? But I thought you didn't believe in love and marriage." Mayur said in disbelief.

"When did I say I don't believe in love and marriage." Ved asked coolly.

"Ever since I remember, you have been saying the same thing again and again, Ved." Karan supported Mayur.

"Well. That was then. This is now." Ved defended himself with a casual shrug of his shoulders.

"Acha?Just like that?" Mayur asked in disbelief.

"Ishq pe hoga yakeen...

ishq ho jaane ke baad." Ved said with a dreamy smile.

Mayur and Karan gaped at him.

"He is saying poetry now," Karan said, sharing a look with Mayur.

"Wait a second. I have heard this somewhere," Mayur said, thinking hard.

Ved tensed at that and cursed himself.

How could he forget the fact that Mayur has the habit of watching daily soaps with Aunt Daya ever since he was a kid.

Does he watch Geet's favourite serial too??

Geet had kept reciting this poetry, the hero of her fav show says, because she just loved it.

And he, who could very well relate to the words too, liked it. And it somehow stuck.

"Yes. It's what the hero says in an ITV show. How do you know this Ved?" Mayur asked, raising an eyebrow at him.

"Leave all that! You tell me what really happened in the cafeteria. What did Tanya tell Geet? She was so scared. It's time to deal with Tanya." Ved said gritting his teeth remembering Geet's tear struck face.

Mayur explained what really happened.

"What are you going to do now? Are you going to fire her?" Karan asked curiously. Ved is a very bad enemy. If you get on his bad side, your life is ruined. There is no second chances in his dictionary.

"Fire her? Of course not. That will be very easy on her. I have other plans. First I need to talk to the HR head." Ved said and dialled the phone to the HR dept.

"Hello. HR Dept, Khuranna Industries." The receptionist answered from the other side.

"It's VK. Ask Svetlana to meet me right now." Ved said and hung up the phone.

Svetlana ,the HR head was in his cabin within five minutes.

"Good afternoon," she greeted the three Khuranna brothers, wondering why she was called upon urgently.

"Take a seat Svetlana. We would like to talk with you regarding some issues," Karan said and Svetlana obliged.

"What is it Sir??" Svetlana asked a bit anxiously.

"It's about Tanya Kapoor," Ved said and Svetlana stiffened.

"Sir, I am really sorry. But I was just doing my job. I had got three complaints about her bullying the juniors. I had to warn her on behalf of the employees Sir." Svetlana said in a rush.

She remembered warning Tanya against bullying ,who in turn just laughed and threatened to get her fired, if she interfered in her matters anymore.

Svetlana knows Tanya holds a higher post in Khurana Industries and she is very good at her job, which makes her almost indispensable.

Ved smirked at the new found information.

Great!! Just great.

"Three employees you said? I would like to see their complaints, Svetlana." Ved said and Karan and Mayur looked at their brother wondering what his plan was.

"But Sir, the complaints are supposed to be confidential. That's the rule of the company." Svetlana said, fearing for the jobs of those three too.

"Do as I said, Svetlana." VK ordered harshly.

"Yes Sir."

"And keep this a secret." VK demanded again.

ᴜre, Sir."

You can leave now."

Svetlana walked out of his cabin cursing Tanya with all the colourful words she know.

Once Svetlana left ,Ved dialled Mr Roy, their legal advisor's number and asked him to get a contract ready.

"What are you planning?" Karan said in exasperation. He doesn't like to be left out of the loop.

"Wait and watch," Ved said with an evil smirk on his face.

. . ❦ . .

EVENING - FIVE PM

Ved wrapped up the work for his day and took his laptop bag ready to leave. As he was about to walk out, the door opened and Mayur barged in.

"I am ready." Mayur said and Ved groaned in annoyance.

"Just go home, Mayur." Ved pleaded.

He didn't want anyone to ruin his alone time with Geet.

"Not happening," Mayur said and at the same time Karan walked in/

"Are you not done yet?" Karan asked ,simultaneously dialling his wife's number.

"Hello Naina. Can you come to..-" Ved snatched his phone away and disconnected the call.

"Karan? Were you going to ask bhabhi to come to the temple?" Ved asked in exasperation.

"Yes. She would also want to meet Geet." Karan said.

"Oh please give me a break," Ved threw his hands up in the air in frustration.

"What is wrong with you?" Karan asked in confusion.

"Nothing is wrong. I don't want everyone at home to know and pressure me into anything. Geet doesn't know my feelings yet. And I don't know if she feels the same. I don't want to overwhelm her by letting the whole family rain down on her." Ved said with an exasperated sigh.

"Okay," Karan said, though not liking the fact that he had to hide it from his wife.

"Please give me some time," Ved pleaded and the brothers could only nod.

Little did he know, Geet's favourite deity had other plans ready for them.

· · ⚜ · ·

The brothers reached the temple premises and Ved looked for Geet at the spot where she usually waits for him. But he didn't find her there today.

"Where did this girl go now?" He asked himself, dialling her number.

She picked up the phone on the fourth ring.

"Yes, Ved ji." She was panting heavily on the other side and Ved got worried instantly.

"Geet? Are you okay? Where are you? Are you hurt? Why do you sound so breathless?" He asked anxiously.

"Uffo Ved ji. I am alright. I am breathless because I have been running. Come to the playground behind the temple." Geet said and hung up without waiting for his response.

He stared at the phone and muttered an 'unbelievable'.

"She is at the playground behind the temple." Ved said and started walking and his brothers followed immediately.

"There is a playground here?" Mayur asked, surprised at that. They all have been here many times, as this is the temple their grandmother and Daya visits often. But they have never noticed a playground here.

"Yeah. There is a shortcut from beside the pond. Or else we will have to drive all the way around to reach the ground." Ved said, now knowing all the nook and corner of the temple.

"How do you know the shortcuts here?" Karan asked curiously.

...r... Geet loves to wander around here and there." He said wardly.

Soon they found Geet on the ground, playing cricket with the kids. More precisely fighting with the kids.

"That was not an Out. The ball didn't touch the bat. Then how can I be out?" Geet argued and her team members supported her while the opposite team argued.

Soon Ved and his brothers stood by her side.

"Let's do one thing. We will start a new game. Now that we have three more players." Geet declared and the brothers looked at her in horror.

"What?" They asked in unison.

"Ved ji in my team." Geet declared happily.

"We want the muscle man bhaiyya," the opposing team demanded and dragged Mayur with him.

"Bade bhaiyya, will you join our team?" Geet asked cutely.

"Uh. I don't actually want to play.." Karan said.

"Bade bhaiyya, please." Geet pleaded with puppy eyes and Karan felt himself melt.

"Okay! One game." Karan agreed.

. . ✦ . .

Inside the temple

The Khuranna ladies offered their prayers and was about to leave, when Naina noticed Karan's car.

"This is Karan's car. Why is he here?" Naina asked, earning the attention of other ladies.

"Call him and see," Ambika said and Naina dialled his number which went unanswered the first time.

The second time she called, she heard the voice of a little girl on the other side.

"Hello, Karan?" She spoke, confused.

"Who is Karan?"

"My husband. This is his phone." Naina said, still confused at who could have attended her husband's phone.

"Oh, that blue eyed uncle?" The little girl asked curiously.

"Yes, and you give the phone to him." Naina asked.

"No. He is batting now. He can't talk." The girl said, shocking Naina.

"Batting?"

"Yes"

"Where is this place?" Naina asked curiously and suspiciously.

"Playground behind Shiv temple." The young girl gave the exact location.

"Okay thank you," a confused Naina said and hung up the call.

"Naina? What happened?" Daya asked.

"I don't know, Mummy ji. She said Karan is batting and is on the ground behind the temple." A confused Naina, let the other ladies also know what the young girl told her.

"That's strange. Let's go and see." Daya said and the three ladies reached the ground only to witness a young girl hugging their rude and arrogant Ved, and jumping up and down in joy.

"Oh my god!"

CHAPTER 8

GEET THREW HER ARMS around Ved's neck and jumped up and down in joy.

"Yay!! We won!" She screamed in excitement.

Ved chuckled seeing her child like excitement at winning street cricket, where it is considered an out if the ball goes out of the boundary. But he loved seeing her smile so widely and heartily. He would do anything to have this smile on her face always.

Mayur wiggled his eyebrows looking at his elder brother only to get a glare in return.

"Geet? Only Ved gets the hug? Even I was on your team. Don't I deserve a hug too?" Karan decided to join his younger brother in teasing.

Geet hearing that, realised what she was doing, and jerked away from Ved, blushing to the roots.

Ved's heart went aww seeing her turning cherry red and he couldn't help but pull her cheeks fondly.

"You are so cute," he said tenderly.

"Aww," his brothers gushed, making Geet blush more.

"I am getting late. I am going home," she said and ran away from there, clutching her heart, which was beating like crazy.

Stupid! Idiot! She chided herself.

How could she hug Ved ji like that in front of everyone? What would they have thought?

Ah ha!! Is it okay to hug him if there was no one around, a voice from inside her asked, making her blush more.

Ved stared at the running figure of Geet and placed his right palm over his heart.

"Hayee..." He sighed dreamily, momentarily forgetting his brothers watching him.

"Aww," the duo chorused again, bringing Ved back from his dreamland.

"Shut up," he glared at them and they laughed out loud.

Karan was still laughing at Ved, but Mayur's laughter died down seeing the sight of Khuranna ladies behind them.

"Ved bhai, Ved bhai!" Mayur hissed in Ved's ears.

"What?" Ved snapped at him for hissing in his ears.

"You are done for, Ved bhai. It's all over!" Mayur said dramatically, making his elder brothers frown at him.

"What?" They both asked, frowning at Mayur's dramatics.

"Turn around and see for yourself." Mayur said.

Ved turned around and cursed under his breath seeing the sight of Khuranna ladies in front of him.

Why God? Why?

"Shall we go home now?" Their grandmother asked sternly and the brothers gulped anxiously.

"Su...sure, dadi."

. . ⚜ . .

Khuranna Mansion

The three brothers came back to the living room, after freshening up, where the ladies were waiting for them/

"Now what are you guys waiting for? Explain!" Their grandmother demanded, looking at her three grandsons.

"Ved bhai wanted to play cricket," Mayur blurted out whatever came to his mind.

"What?"

"Ved bhai, .they are asking you." Mayur nudged his brother.

"Uh dadi.. actually.."

"Leave all that. Tell us about that girl." Daya demanded with twinkling eyes.

"Which girl? We don't know any girl." Mayur said quickly and Ved and Karan nodded their head in unison.

"Oh you already forgot? That girl who was playing with you. The one with proclined teeth and a very ugly smile," Daya asked, making a face.

"Her teeth are perfect and her smile is beautiful." Ved snapped furiously.

"Oh really? But we thought you didn't know any girl." Ambika asked with a cheeky smile and Ved mentally banged his head on the nearby pillar at his foolishness.

"Exactly, mom. This Ved bhai has turned into such a liar. Stop lying bhai . And tell them the truth." Mayur very swiftly changed the team.

"Fine," Ved huffed and proceeded to narrate his love story to his family members.

"And you should have been there at the office this afternoon. It was nothing short of filmy style. I felt as if I was watching a bollywood movie. The heroine being verbally abused by the vamp. Heroine on the verge of crying. Hero's dramatic entry. Heroine flying into hero's arms." Mayur did a dramatic mono act of whatever happened in the office cafe.

"Really? He hugged her in front of all his employees?" Daya asked excited. They were all finding it hard to believe. Because it was Ved. Ved Khuranna, who never believed in love and marriages. And the same Ved Khuranna is now standing in front of them, all besotted and whipped.

Geet Jha! What magic did you do on our Ved? All the minds were asking the same question.

Ved groaned mentally planning to murder his younger brother for blurting out everything.

"And you know what she called him?" Mayur asked cheekily.

"Shut up, Mayur. That's enough." Ved chided, but he was royally ignored by everyone.

"You continue," Naina said, her imaginary popcorn in her hands.

"She calls him Ved jiiiiiiii." Mayur said exaggerating the jiiii.

"Aww," Naina cooed and Ved looked down awkwardly.

"How could you hide this from us, Ved Khuranna. Daya, Ambika get the shagun ready. We will go there tomorrow itself." Dadi declared and the brothers looked at her in horror.

"For heaven's sake, this is exactly why I didn't want to tell you all." Ved snapped angrily.

"Why not?" Ambika frowned at her son. She was always worried that her wrong decisions and failed marriage would lead to Ved ending up alone in life, not believing in relationships and marriage. But now she is relieved.

"Let us get to know each other first, Maa. Let her get used to me. Let her be more comfortable with me." Ved said and his brothers gaped at him.

"She hugged you. You kissed her. How much more comfortable are you talking about?" Karan asked as the ladies shrieked.

"You kissed her?" Naina asked, her eyes wide in excitement and curiosity.

Ved groaned in exasperation.

"This discussion is over. There will be no talks of marriage proposal anytime soon. When the time is right, I will let you all know."

. . ❦ . .

Ved picked up the call as soon as the phone rang.

"Geet..."

"Ved ji..." Geet whispered anxiously.

"What happened Geet?"

"Maya bua is coming, Vedji.." Geet whispered

"Papa's elder sister?" Ved asked, vaguely recalling Geet talking about her aunt who lives in the city.

"Yes."

"What's the problem? She is your aunt, right?" Ved asked curiously.

"Yes yes. I don't mind her coming. But she doesn't come alone, Ved ji." Geet huffed in annoyance.

"Who does she bring with her?"

"Advice!"

"What??"

"She comes along with a speech on how I should be married off as quickly as possible." Geet said in annoyance.

"What?" Ved yelled through the phone.

"Why are you shouting Ved ji. I can hear very well."

"Marriage? They are marrying you off?" Ved asked in disbelief.

"I don't know. Save me Ved ji," Geet pleaded as if she was being married off the very next day.

"I will," Ved promised, imagining himself as her knight in shining armour.

"Thank you, thank you, thank you so much."

"Mmm.."

"Okay. Let me sleep. I have to wake up early tomorrow morning as Bua is coming." Geet said.

"Okay. Good night."

Ved paced the room like a caged tiger.

How could they marry her off just like that?

What will he do?

He walked out of the room to find the ladies of his family along with Mayur watching TV.

"Listen.." He called out to no one in particular.

"What?"

"I am ready," he said, making them frown.

"Ready for what?"

"Shagun. Let's go tomorrow morning itself. I don't want any more delay."

"Oh my god!!"

CHAPTER 9

VED WOKE UP EARLIER than usual and waited for the ladies to finish their morning prayers.

"Ah ha! Seems like someone is up so early today." Naina teased, to which he rolled his eyes impatiently.

"We need to plan things," Ved said in a serious tone.

"What is there to plan?" Daya asked in a disinterested tone.

"Aunt Daya.." Ved whined.

Ved Khuranna whined, surprising everyone.

"Okay, okay. Let's talk." Ambika said with a soft smile.

"We will leave soon after breakfast. Under no circumstances you are to say Geet and I already know each other. I sent her a whatsapp message regarding the same. She hasn't seen it yet. But I guess she is still asleep. So, as I was saying, the story would be like, you all saw her at the temple, you all liked her. So we are taking the proposal. Got it?" Ved asked.

"Hold on! Why should we lie?? We can say you both met at the temple, talked to each other and liked each other. What's wrong with it??" Naina asked in confusion.

"Bhabhi, they just recently moved from their village. These things are common in cities. Not in villages. I don't know how Papa would react if he comes to know we have been in contact for all these days. What if he thinks I have been trying to spoil his daughter?" Ved asked anxiously.

"Have you been?" Daya asked, narrowing her eyes suspiciously at him.

"What?"

"Have you been trying to spoil her, Ved?"

"Come on Aunt.. We just talk. Mostly about her television serials or that old hag Sharukh Khan." Ved said grudgingly remembering all the instances where Geet used to gush over the fifty year old man.

"Don't tell me you are jealous of Sharukh Khan." Naina said, laughing at him.

"Of course not"

"Oh god! You really are jealous of Sharukh Khan because your Geet is a Sharukh Khan fan?" Naina asked in disbelief and Ved felt his cheeks heating up in embarrassment.

"Bhabhi, focus on the matter now." Ved said in exasperation.

"Okay fine. We will go with your story." Dadi agreed.

"And yeah. One more thing," Ved said awkwardly.

"Yeah??" Everyone looked at him curiously.

"Just- just try to make a good impression about me." Ved said looking at the pattern of the carpet very seriously.

"What?" The ladies laughed

"Come on. Her papa somehow thinks that I am arrogant and rude." Ved said sulkily.

"Uh. That you are." Ambika pointed out cheekily.

"But I am not rude with Geet. I have never been and never will." Ved vowed, making the ladies smile.

"Aww," came the chorus from the ladies.

"So everything is set. We will leave after breakfast." Ved said, excited.

"No. We can't simply barge into someone's house and ask for their daughter's hand, Ved. There are certain formalities for that." Dadi said, making Ved frown.

"Leave it to us. We will manage." Dadi said.

"How?"

"Daya, you have the contact number of the priest's house?" Dadi asked.

"Ji Mummy." Daya said and dialled the number instantly.

The priest's wife answered the call and Kalyani Khuranna talked in length about how they found the perfect match for their Ved at the temple. And went in detail about the girl, whom the other lady identified easily.

The pandit's wife informed the pandit about the alliance who in turn contacted Shukla ji, the house owner, to get more information about the family who recently moved into their colony.

The pandit talked with Haresh Jha about the Khuranna family's interest, shocking them.

In short, within an hour Kalyani Khuranna was on call with Mr and Mrs Jha, requesting whether they could come to their house to talk in detail.

The shocked Jhas, prompted by the infamous Maya bua ,said yes, making the junior Jha glare at her aunt from behind her.

"Done," Kalyani said smugly.

"Dadi, you are simply awesome." Mayur who had by then joined them along with Karan said.

"Why do you think you dada ji was hell bent on marrying me? Simply because I am awesome." Kalyani said smugly.

At the same moment Ved received a message from Mr Roy, their legal advisor and he smirked.

"So we will leave only in the afternoon right? I will be back from the office by then."

"But I thought you would take a day off today?" Ambika complained.

"Something important came up." Ved said vaguely.

"We thought Geet is more important now," Naina said, raising an eyebrow at him challengingly.

"She is. And that's why I have to go to the office now. There is some unfinished business to take care of." Ved said with a smirk and Karan and Mayur understood what the business is.

"We will also come with you," Karan said to which Ved shrugged.

. . ∽ . .

Geet was sulking ever since they received the phone call from the Khuranna matriarch.

How could her papa do this to her?

Wasn't he the one who told her that VK is rude and arrogant.

Then how could they even think about marrying her off to this arrogant VK.

Geet glared at Maya who was turning her cupboard upside down searching for an outfit for her to wear today.

She couldn't even talk to Ved ji about this.

How could she, when Maya bua have been tagging her along ever since she came.

Only if she could give a hint to Ved ji, he would have come to her rescue as he promised.

And Ved ji works for VK. Maybe Ved ji can talk to VK ji and explain.

But how to make a call to Ved ji?

"Geet. You will wear this saree. It will look good on you." Maya said, taking out a chiffon saree out of the cupboard.

She sent a pleading look at her mother who always goes silent in the presence of her intimidating sister in law.

"They are big people, Geet. We can't simply refuse them and hurt their egos. Let them come and go. And if you didn't like them, we will find some excuses," her mother whispered in her ears, understanding her daughter's plight.

"Thank you, momma. I don't want to marry VK ji." Geet said in relief.

"You don't have to marry anyone you don't like." Nalini said fondly.

"Nalini..." Maya called out.

"Yes, didi."

"Do you have some jewels that could go with the saree?" Maya asked.

"Yes, didi."

"Good. It is a very good proposal. Something we can't even dream about. Do you have any idea who the Khurannas are? Girls all over

Mumbai are dying to marry one of them and they want our Geet. Thank our lucky stars." Maya said, making Geet frown.

"Why would anyone be lucky to marry a rude and arrogant man. Strange!" Geet mumbled to herself.

Haresh Jha came inside the room.

"They said they will be here in one hour." He informed his family.

"Hey Ram!! What are you waiting for girl? Go go!! Take a quick shower." Maya pushed her into the bathroom, making Geet grumble under her breath.

· · ༄ · ·

CHAPTER 10

AS SOON AS HE REACHED the office, Ved asked his secretary to send Sventlana, the HR head in.

Svetlana came in, cursing Tanya in all the colourful profanities she knew.

"Good morning, Sir." Svetlana greeted the Khuranna brothers.

"Good morning, Svetlana. Let me get straight to the point. I want the names of the three juniors in the PR department who complained against Tanya." Ved demanded.

"Yes, sir." Svetlana gulped and forwarded the list to VK.

"Payal Gupta, Preetika Sharma and Aastha Kirloskar. Good. You can leave now, Svetlana." VK dismissed Svetlana and summoned Tanya after getting the contract papers from Mr Roy.

"VK. You asked for me??" Tanya simpered, making Ved grit his teeth.

Ved clenched his fist to stop himself from strangling the witch for making his Geet cry.

"Take a seat, Tanya." Mayur said and Tanya did as asked.

"Ms Kapoor. You are already aware of the new government tender. I want you to work for it." Ved said.

"Of course VK. Do you need to ask??" Tanya asked in a sultry voice, making the brothers cringe.

"And you have to sign a contract. This deal is very important for the company so we are not taking any chances. You can read the contract well and can sign only if you are ready." Ved said and passed on the contract papers to her.

Tanya frowned upon reading the contract.

It says she has to pay a compensation of five crores if she leaves the work half way through. But then, she never leaves any work half way. So that is not an issue.

She will have to report to the person assigned by the Khuranna brothers. That is usual. They always keep a head for each deal. Mostly Mr Mishra or Mr Mathur.

"Sure. I will sign the deal." Tanya said without a second thought.

"Are you sure? Read the contract properly. It is water tight." Ved said.

"Yeah, I understand." Tanya said and signed the contract immediately.

Ved smirked. He passed the signed documents to his lawyers and asked them to register in immediately. And his highly paid team of lawyers did the job effectively immediately.

Ved picked up the intercom and called his PA.

"Send Payal Gupta, Preetika Sharma and Aastha Kirloskar in." Ved said and hung up the call.

Tanya smirked. The trio are her slaves in the department.

The three women came in sweating profusely as Svetlana Ma'am had already informed them about VK asking about the complaints.

Ved passed another file towards them.

"Read and sign them." Ved ordered.

The three of them read the contract and stared at VK gobsmacked.

"Yes?" VK asked, raising an eyebrow.

"Sir. This says we are to head the PR campaign for the government tender." Aastha said, confused.

"Yes. That's what it says. Do you have a problem with that?" Ved said

"What? How is that possible? I am the PR head." Tanya said, frowning.

"Not anymore," Ved said, relishing the look on Tanya's face.

"What?"

"You will be reporting to the three ladies here from today onwards.." Ved said.

"They are my juniors," Tanya thundered angrily.

"I just promoted them. Now you are their junior." Ved said, shrugging.

"I refuse to do this. I am resigning from the job." Tanya stood up furiously.

"Sure, you are free to resign after paying the compensation of ten crores." Ved smirked.

Tanya stared at him in horror.

Why didn't she see this coming?

"This is about that girl. Isn't it??" Tanya asked, finally catching up with what is happening around.

Ved looked at her coldly.

"Ma'am," he uttered, confusing her.

"What??"

"Not that girl, this girl and all. Call her Ma'am. Geet Ma'am. Or GK, soon. Geet Khuranna." Ved declared and all the four women in the cabin stared at him.

Ved turned to the trio.

"Are you signing the contract? Or is it that you don't want a promotion?" Ved asked.

"Of course sir. We are signing." The three said and signed the contract, trying hard to stifle their grin.

·· ❧ ··

"Nalini, I think they reached." Haresh Jha said to his wife.

"Oh, I will see if Geet is ready," Nalini said and walked into Geet's room where Maya Bua was helping her get ready.

Nalini stopped short seeing her daughter in a peach coloured saree with red and golden borders.

Her daughter was wearing a simple antique jewel that belonged to her late mother in law.

Both her hands are filled with glass bangles, a mix of peach red and gold.

When did she grow up?

Nalini felt her eyes fill up with tears.

The thought of marrying her off filled her heart with an ache.

But then parents with daughters would always feel that ache.

"Geet...??" Geet looked up to see her mother in tears and frowned.

"What happened momma? Why are you crying?" Geet asked anxiously.

"You are all grown up. And you look so gorgeous." Nalini said, warding off evil eyes with her hands.

"I am sure the Khurannas would want to take her away with them right away." Maya teased, making Geet frown more.

"You aren't marrying me off today, are you momma?" Geet whispered to her mother.

Nalini smiled fondly at her daughter

"I just came in to check if you are ready. They reached. Let me go and welcome them."

Geet prayed hard for a miracle to happen.

How could she marry VK ji when she wants to marry Vedji.

Her eyes widened realising what she just thought.

Marry Ved ji??

The thought made her blush hard.

"Aww. My niece is shy. Look at your daughter blushing, Nalini." Maya teased again and Geet looked away.

She wasn't blushing for VK ji coming to see her. She was blushing for her Ved ji.

Ved along with his family entered the Jha house and was warmly welcomed by the Jha couple.

Ved bent down to touch his future in laws' feet leaving his family to gape at him.

"Oh my god!" Daya whispered in her sister in law's ears, earning an elbow nudge in return.

"Bless you, son." The surprised Jha couple blessed the prospective groom.

Haresh stared at the tall and well built haired man in wonder.

He had been going to the Khuranna Industries for a while now and all he had heard about the two elder brothers was that they are arrogant, rude and ruthless.

But the man in front of him looks very cultured and softspoken.

Maybe a tad bit too cultured.

How is that possible?

"Please have your seat," Haresh said, welcoming the Khurannas to get settled.

The Khurannas took their seats and exchanged pleasantries with the Jhas.

"We saw Geet beta at the temple," Dadi began following the script.

"Ji. She is always at the temple nowadays." Haresh said, truthfully.

When they were in the village, Geet used to visit the temple twice a week. But for the past one month, she has been at the temple almost all the time.

"This is my second grandson, Ved. We are here to ask for your daughter's hand for him." Dadi said with a smile.

"Ji. I have heard about him," Haresh said and Ved tensed.

Daya chuckled seeing Ved's expression.

"Uh oh! I am sure you have only heard bad things about him. But they are all rumours. Our Ved is twenty four karat pure gold." Daya said dramatically and Ved cursed himself for asking his family to create a good image of him.

He should have known his crazy family would only make it worse by overdoing it.

"Aunt," Ved smiled at his aunt, though the look in his eyes were a warning.

"Yeah. I have heard things about him in the office. We deliver the food to the canteen there." Haresh said.

"It is- it is difficult to run the company and we have to be strict, else the company would suffer." Ved defended himself.

"I understand." Haresh said with a smile.

"Where is Geet?" Ambika asked, eager to meet the girl who stole her son's heart so easily.

"I will go get her." Nalini said and walked inside to bring Geet.

Ved felt his heart thudding against his ribs.

He hasn't heard her voice today. And he has been missing her like crazy.

They all looked up at the sound of the anklet and Ved felt all breath leave his lungs at once.

Geet was always gorgeous.

But Geet in saree is simply stunning.

His eyes traced every beautiful line of hers.

She hasn't looked up yet.

Haresh Jha looked at Ved and saw him look at Geet like, Geet look at pani puris?

He frowned. Soon the frown was replaced by confusion when he heard his daughter's cheerful squeal

"Ved jiiii."

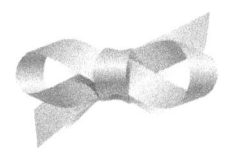

CHAPTER 11

"VED JIIIII," GEET SQUEALED happily, seeing him sitting there.

Ved face palmed. She oh so graciously poured cold water over his plans of a perfect arranged marriage set up.

Geet grinned ear to ear.

He came. He really came as promised.

He came to rescue her from VK ji.

How sweet her Ved ji is!!

Now all she has to do is ask Ved ji to tell her parents and aunt how much of a brute this VK is.

Geet looked around and found the people she had seen in the photo Ved ji had shown her yesterday.

She hadn't recognised bade bhaiyya and Mayur bhaiyya though she had heard about them a lot. So she wanted to see them all and so he had shown her a family photo telling her who is who.

She bent down and took blessings from Dadi, Ambika and Daya.

The senior Jhas stared at their daughter in shock.

"Geet you know them?" Haresh asked in shock.

"Yes papa. Ved ji is my friend. We met at the temple." Geet informed, happily.

"Why didn't you tell us before?" Nalini whispered furiously.

"Because Ved ji wanted me to hide it. Now he himself came here, so there is no need to hide anymore," she said and Ved clutched his heart in panic.

"What?" Haresh asked, glaring at Ved who refused to look at him.

"Ved ji. Tell them not to marry me off to VK ji" Geet presented her major worry to Ved who looked at his family helplessly.

"What are you talking about, Geet. You said he is your friend and yet you don't know who he is?" Maya asked in confusion.

"He is Ved ji." Geet declared in simple words.

"And who do you think is VK??" Haresh asked patiently, realising that his daughter is not aware of it.

Ved stared at Geet with his heart in his mouth.

How would she react? Will she be angry at him? Will she hate him for fooling her?

"VK ji is the boss of that big company where Ved ji works. Everyone says he is a bad man. Everyone is scared of him. Papa, you told me that day when I went there with the food, that I should stay out of his way. And now you are thinking of marrying me off to him." Geet asked bravely.

Her Vedji is with her now and he had promised her to save her. So there is no need to worry about Maya bua's anger.

Haresh glared at Ved for fooling his daughter.

"Geet.." Ved called out softly.

"Yes, Ved ji." Geet smiled at him and his heart fluttered again.

"I am VK, Geet." He said and Geet frowned in confusion.

"What? I don't understand, Ved ji" Geet said, confused.

"My name is Ved Khuranna. VK in short." Ved said.

"How could you?" Geet asked angrily, her hands on her hips.

"Geet, I can explain. I didn't want to lie to you..." He began to explain, but Geet cut him off mid way.

"How could you not tell me you are VK. And how could they all say you are rude and arrogant. If I had known you were VK, I would have told my papa then, that you are the sweetest and kindest man on the earth." Geet said and Ved gaped at her.

"What?"

"And that vampire, I mean Tanya ji. She was trying to scare me by saying your name. Huh!! If I had known my Ved ji is VK, I would have taught her a lesson then and there itself." Geet said, the thought of missing a golden chance filling her with regret.

"Could someone tell us what is happening here?" Haresh asked, impatiently.

"Haresh ji. My grandson met your daughter at a temple a few weeks ago. They got to know each other and became good friends. And when he told us about her, we thought we would ask for her hand." Dadi said, trying for a quick damage control.

Geet grinned at Ved.

"You want to marry me, Ved ji?" She asked happily.

"Yes," Ved mumbled, feeling all eyes on him.

"Do you love me, Ved ji??" Geet asked directly, ignoring the scandalised gasp from her parents and aunt.

Ved felt his ears and cheeks heating up.

"Geet..." He whispered, pleading with her to shut up.

"Tell me, Ved ji.." Geet whined.

"Yes," Ved whispered.

"Pyaar wala love?" Geet asked.

"Haa!"

"Mohabbat wala love?" She asked.

"Haa!"

"Ishq wala love?" She asked again.

"Haa."

"Me too, Ved ji. Me too." Geet declared excitedly and hugged her mother and kissed her cheeks loudly.

"She is not usually like this." Maya said embarrassed at the way Geet was behaving. She was now sure they were going to reject Geet after her shameless behaviour.

"I love her the way she is Bua." Ved said strongly, looking straight at the older woman.

"She can be a little childish at times. Responsibility of being a daughter in law is big. Geet is too young for that." Haresh said and Geet frowned.

"Papa..."

"Let me talk, Geet."

"I understand your worries, papa. I will take care of her and help her adjust to the new life." Ved promised.

"She will not be a daughter in law for us. She will be our daughter." Ambika promised.

Soon the Shagun ceremony was held and the Khurannas showered Geet with gifts.

And the neighbours too started to drop in to see their Geet bitiya's groom.

"Damad ji. I am Balraj Gupta. I have a pani puri stall around the corner. Come with Geet bitiya when you get time." Gupta chacha said followed by Shukla chacha, Mishra kaka, Vimala mausi, Kamala chachi and the numerous neighbouring uncles and aunties who wanted a piece of their new damad ji.

(Damad ji - son in law)

Ved sighed in relief when all of them left him alone.

Mayur laughed, seeing his elder brother's plight.

"What?"

"You had a problem in being the son in law of one family. Look at you. You became the son in law of a whole housing colony. How cute!" Mayur teased.

"Shut up, Mayur."

. . ✿ . .

Night

"Hello Ved ji.." Geet greeted cheerfully.

"Geet..." Ved uttered her name contentedly.

Finally she's his!!

"You know Ved ji.. I was so worried in the morning thinking about getting married to VK ji" Geet laughed.

"And now??" Ved asked.

"I am so happy I am marrying my Ved ji." Geet declared happily.

"I love you, Geet."

"I too love you so much, Ved ji."

CHAPTER 12 - EPILOGUE

VED HELD GEET'S HAND when they walked into the ballroom.

It was a cocktail party arranged for the employees of Khuranna Industries. Their wedding is to be held in a week.

The wedding is happening in full Punjabi style, except for this cocktail party.

After the small Shagun ceremony held at Geet's home the day they went to ask her hand for marriage, they did the roka ceremony two days later.

He had gifted her a set of diamond studs that day.

She was wearing them tonight, which complements well with the turquoise cocktail gown she is wearing.

This was the first time he saw Geet in western style. And she looked absolutely gorgeous in it.

"Geet, you look gorgeous." He whispered to her as they walked in.

Geet gave him a bright smile in return.

"And you are the most handsome man I have ever met, Ved ji" Geet complimented him openly.

He had bought her this gown, because he loved that colour on her.

For their chunni ceremony, she was wearing a turquoise coloured lehenga with the same coloured choli with extensive baby pink embroidery on it.

They conducted the engagement on the same day evening, where they exchanged rings, officially committing to each other.

Ved walked around with Geet, introducing her to business associates and other employees.

"Ved ji. I am tired." Geet huffed after walking around for a while.

"Let's sit here." Ved guided her to a couch in the corner.

"Oh!! That feels like heaven." Geet mumbled, removing her high heels, which her Maya bua forced her to wear.

"I will go get something for you to drink." Ved said sweetly.

"Thank you, Ved ji. I am really thirsty." Geet said in gratitude.

As soon as Ved was out of sight, Tanya walked towards Geet, her eyes spitting envy.

"You are the middle class girl who trapped VK." Tanya gritted out giving Geet a once over.

Geet looked at Tanya bored.

"Yes. That's me!!" Geet said cooly.

"Well. Let's see how long you will be able to hold his attention." Tanya smirked.

"Are you going to keep a watch on us? You don't have any work at the office?" Geet asked, making Tanya fume.

"You illiterate fool. Do you even know what you are getting into? He is just hooked to the novelty of you. Once the novelty wears off, he will come back to me." Tanya said in an evil tone.

"You? Why would he come back to you? Who are you anyways?" Geet asked curiously, wondering why this woman has such stupid beliefs.

"Because that's how rich people are." Tanya gritted out.

Geet laughed heartily.

"Why are you laughing?"

"I always wanted to have my love story like they show in my serials. But my Ved ji is so sweet. There was no drama. At least I had a vamp in my story." Geet said happily.

"What the hell?? Did you just call me a vamp?" Tanya asked in disbelief.

She wanted to create trouble for what Ved did to her. She thought the village bumpkin would run off crying.

Geet sighed

"Tanya ji. Why do you want to be a vamp in my story? You look good. You have a good job. You are smart. If you try, you can be a heroine in your own story. After all, what do you even lack?" Geet asked in utter confusion.

Ved who saw Tanya near Geet had rushed back to them and that's when he heard Geet's dialogue.

He couldn't stop the smirk from forming on his face.

"Exactly Tanya. What do you even lack? Haa!! After tonight, you will be lacking a proper job." Ved said, informing her she is no more welcome at the Khuranna Industries.

Tanya walked away fuming.

She was not worried about the job. She was demoted and she didn't particularly want the job anymore. She couldn't resign because she will have to pay the compensation. So she thought she could at least create some misunderstanding between the couple, but she failed miserably.

Ved handed over the cool drink to Geet.

"Geet. Don't take her seriously."

"Don't worry Ved ji. I have seen a similar scene before." Geet said excitedly.

"In your serial?" Ved asked indulgently.

"No. I read it in a story. Actually there are so many good stories on many online platforms. They are so freaking amazing. Better than the television shows." Geet said excitedly.

"Really?"

"And you know Ved ji. I found a story written by one of these amazing writers. The Sheikh's Unforgettable Wife. That's the story's name. In that story, the hero and the heroine have a set of triplets. And they are so cute. I love all three of them. I hope we also get triplets after marriage." Geet said dreamily.

"Ah ha! You want to have babies, Geet?" Ved asked huskily.

Geet blushed.

Reading these stories on online platforms has been very informative. They write things they don't show in the television shows and movies.

Suffice to say, she prefers reading novels over watching her serial now.

Does that make her a bad girl? Because she like reading stuff like that?

"Are you blushing, Geet?" Ved asked huskily and Geet's breath hitched.

He leaned forwards and her breathing quickened.

Is he going to kiss her? Like the hero in the story she read in the morning.

In the story, the triplets come running from nowhere whenever the hero is near the heroine. But there is no one here to interrupt them.

Ved stared at her heaving form. His eyes zeroed in on her lips. He badly wanted to kiss her.

Geet parted her lips instinctively. She darted her tongue out and licked her lips as they went dry suddenly.

Ved groaned and pulled back, controlling himself.

"Geet. Let's go. Everyone will be waiting for us."

"Oh," Geet mumbled disappointedly.

. . ༄ . .

"What do you mean by I can't attend the function??" Ved asked in exasperation.

"Men are not allowed for the mehndi function, Ved." Ambika said calmly.

"Why not?? I am the one getting married. How can you say that I can't attend my own pre wedding ritual?" Ved asked in disbelief.

"That's the custom, Ved." Dadi said.

"That's unfair." Ved complained.

"You can attend the sangeet ceremony tomorrow." Daya said, trying to placate him.

"Oh!! How nice of you, to let me attend my own function." Ved said sarcastically.

After the Khuranna women left, Ved was pacing back and forth in the poolside, bitching about the old customs.

"Will you stop it? I am getting a headache watching you pace like this." Mayur said in annoyance.

"I am going." Ved declared suddenly.

"Where?" Karan asked casually, sipping on his coffee.

"To Geet's house." Ved said, walking out and Karan and Mayur had to run ro keep up with him.

"You can't go there." Karan called out to him.

"Why not? I am sure they will welcome their damad ji wholeheartedly." Ved said smugly, knowing how much the people in the area already loved their Geet bitiya's fiance.

True to his words,Ved was welcomed into the function with hugs from the men and pinches on his cheeks and chin from the women.

Ved ignored the glares from the Khuranna women and sat next to Geet.

"Ved ji. You came!!" Geet said excitedly.

"How can I miss seeing my Geet getting her mehndi done." Ved asked, flicking her nose playfully.

The mehndi artist giggled as she continued with the design.

"Is my name written there?" Ved whispered to Geet.

Geet nodded in no and Ved's smile dimmed.

"I was lying. Your name is hidden in the design." Geet said cheekily.

"Ah ha! Do you think I should also get your name written in my palms?" Ved asked curiously.

"Will you??" Geet asked, her eyes sparkling with excitement.

"Anything for you Geet." Ved said and got another mehndi artist to write Geet's name on his palm.

The Sangeet ceremony was held at Geet's place itself.

A makeshift stage was made in the street.

The opening dance was by their dadi, who danced on a fast number leaving the audience gaping.

The next dance was performed by Ambika Daya and Nalini together.

The next dance was by Karan and Naina. They were dancing on an old bollywood number.

Ved gaped at Karan who was wearing a shirt with green and yellow floral print.

If their business associates sees this dance, they will never take KK seriously again.

The function ended with a dance by Geet and Ved on the song 'Suraj Hua Mad ham' from the famous Sharukh Khan movie Kabhi Khushi Kabhi Ghum.

. . ॐ . .

"For heaven sake. Keep my credit card and get whatever you want," Ved huffed in annoyance, trying to get past Naina to go to his bedroom where his newly wedded wife is waiting for him.

"Credit card?? Is it unlimited?" Naina asked cheekily.

"Yes yes. Buy whatever you want." Ved said impatiently.

Naina finally took pity on him and let him inside the room.

His heart drummed against his rib cage at the sight of Geet sitting on the centre of their bed with her vein covering her face.

She looked ethereal.

"Geet," he whispered, raising the veil.

"Ved ji. Why were you late?" She pouted cutely.

"I am here now." Ved whispered.

Geet hugged him tightly.

"We are married, Ved ji. We are married," she squealed in excitement.

"Yes. We are." Ved chuckled happily.

He helped her in removing her ornaments and the numerous hairpins that held her long thick hair together.

As soon as her hair fell down her back, Geet sighed in relief.

Ved gently massaged her head and a moan of pleasure escaped Geet's lips.

Ved gulped hearing her moan.

"That feels good." Geet mumbled in pleasure.

Ved continued gently massaging her hair.

"Ved ji, can you untie the strings of my blouse. It's too tight." Geet said and Ved gulped as he moved her hair over her shoulders.

Her milky white back got exposed to him. He wanted to kiss every inch of her satiny soft skin.

He untied the strings that held together the blouse, other than the single hook.

"There are marks," Ved said and he caressed the reddish marks made by the tight thread on her skin.

Geet stiffened feeling his caress.

She quickly turned around and hugged him shyly.

"Geet..." He called her and placed a finger on her chin, raising her head.

He caressed her cheeks lovingly and Geet's arms crept around his neck unknowingly.

Ved bent down a little and looked into her eyes to see if she felt any discomfort.

When he saw she was waiting for him to proceed, he leaned in and took her lips in his.

He sucked in her lower lip and Geet mimicked his actions.

"I love you, Geet." Ved mumbled into her mouth.

"I too love you, Ved ji."

. . ⚘ . .

THE END

About the Author

Dr. Sirin Fathima is a dentist by profession and a writer by passion. A lifelong avid reader, she recently discovered her love for storytelling and has since become a celebrated author in the romance genre. Known for her ability to craft light-hearted romantic novels with a perfect blend of emotion, humour, and moderate steam, Dr. Sirin's stories always promise a happy-ever-after.

With over ten romance novels and numerous short stories to her credit, her works have garnered a loyal readership on various online platforms. Now, she's set to embark on an exciting new chapter with the release of her first paperback novel, bringing her captivating characters and heartfelt tales to an even broader audience.

Milton Keynes UK
Ingram Content Group UK Ltd.
UKHW042031031224
452078UK00001B/53